Bernard Shaw

This is the Preachment on Going to Church

Bernard Shaw

This is the Preachment on Going to Church

ISBN/EAN: 9783337162764

Printed in Europe, USA, Canada, Australia, Japan

Cover: Foto ©Andreas Hilbeck / pixelio.de

More available books at **www.hansebooks.com**

THIS IS THE PREACHMENT•••
ON GOING TO CHURCH•••WRIT
BY GEORGE BERNARD SHAW
AND DONE INTO PRINT AT THE
ROYCROFT PRINTING SHOP ❦
WHICH IS IN EAST AURORA,
NEW YORK, U. S. A. ❦❦❦

MDCCCXCVI

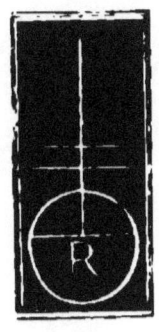

ON GOING TO CHURCH.

I

O ME, as a modern man, concerned with matters of fine art and living in London by the sweat of my brain, 'tis a grim fact that I dwell in a world which, unable to live by bread alone, lives spiritually on alcohol and morphia ❧ Young and excessively sentimental city people live on love, and delight in poetry or fine writing which declares that love is Alpha and Omega. But an attentive examination will generally establish the fact that this kind of love, ethereal as it seems, is merely a symptom of the drugs I have mentioned, and does not occur independently except in those persons whose normal state is similar to that induced in healthy persons by narcotic stimulants ❧ If from the fine art of to-day we set aside feelingless or prosaic

I

art, which is, properly, not fine art at all, we may safely refer most of the rest to feeling produced by the teapot, the bottle, or the hypodermic syringe ❧

An exhibition of the cleverest men and women in London at five p. m., with their afternoon tea cut off, would shatter many illusions. Tea and coffee and cigarettes produce conversation; lager beer and pipes produce routine journalism; wine and gallantry produce brilliant journalism, essays and novels; brandy and cigars produce violently devotional or erotic poetry; morphia produces tragic exaltation (useful on the stage); and sobriety produces an average curate's sermon.

AGAIN, strychnine and arsenic may be taken as pick-me-ups; doctors quite understand that "tonics" mean drams of ether; chlorodyne is a universal medicine; chloral, sulphonal and the like call up Nature's great

2

destroyer, artificial sleep ; bromide of potassium will reduce the over-sensitive man of genius to a condition in which the alighting of a wasp on his naked eyeball will not make him wink ; hasheesh tempts the dreamer by the Oriental glamour of its reputation ; and gin is a cheap substitute for all these anodynes ✤ Most of the activity of the Press, the Pulpit, the Platform and the Theatre is only a sympton of the activity of the drug trade, the tea trade, the tobacco trade and the liquor trade. The world is not going from bad to worse, it is true ; but the increased facilities which constitute the advance of civilization include facilities for drugging one's self. These facilities wipe whole races of black men off the face of the earth ; and every extension and refinement of them picks a stratum out of white society and devotes it to destruction. Such traditions of the gross old habits as have reached me seem to be based on the idea of first doing your day's work and then enjoying yourself by getting drunk 🌿 Nowadays you get drunk to enable you to begin work.

SHAKESPERE'S opportunities of meddling with his nerves were much more limited than Dante Rossetti's; but it is not clear that the advantages of the change lay with Rossetti. Besides, though Shakespere may, as tradition asserts, have died of drink in a ditch, he at all events conceived alcohol as an enemy put by a man into his own mouth to steal away his brains; whereas the modern man conceives it as an indispensable means of setting his brains going. We drink and drug, not for the pleasure of it, but for Dutch inspiration and by the advice of our doctors, as duelists drink for Dutch courage by the advice of their seconds 🌿 Obviously this systematic, utilitarian drugging and stimulating, though necessarily "moderate" (so as not to defeat its own object), is more dan-

4

gerous than the old boozing if we are to regard the use of stimulants as an evil.

S for me, I do not clearly see where a scientific line can be drawn between food and stimulants. I cannot say, like Ninon de l'Enclos, that a bowl of soup intoxicates me; but it stimulates me as much as I want to be stimulated, which is, perhaps, all that Ninon meant. Still, I have not failed to observe that all the drugs, from tea to morphia, and all the drams, from lager beer to brandy, dull the edge of self-criticism and make a man content with something less than the best work of which he is soberly capable ❧ He thinks his work better, when he is really only more easily satisfied with himself. Those whose daily task is only a routine, for the sufficient discharge of which a man need hardly be more than half alive, may seek this fool's paradise without detriment to their work; but to those professional men whose art affords practically boundless scope for skill of execution and elevation of thought, to take drug or dram is to sacrifice the keenest, most precious part of life to — a dollop of lazy and vulgar comfort for which no true man of genius should have any greater stomach than the lady of the manor has for her ploughman's lump of fat bacon.

FOR the creative artist stimulants are especially dangerous, since they produce that terrible dream-glamour in which the ugly, the grotesque, the wicked, the morbific begin to fascinate and obsess instead of disgusting. This effect, however faint it may be, is always produced in some degree by drugs. The mark left on a novel in the " Leisure Hour " by a cup of tea may be imperceptible to a bishop's wife who has just had two cups; but the effect is there as certainly as if De Quincey's eight thousand drops of laudanum had been substituted.

6

TO CHURCH.

II

ONLY a very little experience of the world of art and letters will convince any open-minded person that abstinence, pure and simple, is not a practicable remedy for this state of things. There is a considerable commercial demand for maudlin or nightmarish art and literature which no sober person would produce, the manufacture of which must accordingly be frankly classed industrially with the unhealthy trades, and morally with the manufacture of unwholesome sweets for children or the distilling of gin. What the victims of this industry call imagination and artistic faculty is nothing but attenuated delirium tremens, like Pasteur's attenuated hydrophobia. It is useless to encumber an argument with these predestined children of perdition. The only profitable cases are those to consider of people engaged in the healthy pursuit of those arts which afford scope for the greatest mental and physical energy, the clearest and acutest reason and the most elevated perception. Work of this kind requires an intensity of energy of which no ordinary labourer or routine official can form any conception. If the dreams of Keeleyism could be so far realized as to transmute human brain energy into vulgar explosive force, the head of Shakespere, used as a bombshell, might conceivably blow England out of the sea. At all events, the succession of efforts by which a Shaksperean play, a Beethoven symphony, or a Wagner music-drama is produced, though it may not overtax Shakespere, Beethoven or Wagner, must certainly tax even them to the utmost, and would be as prodigiously impossible to the average professional man as the writing of an ordinary leading article to a ploughman.

TO CHURCH.

HAT is called professional work is, in point of severity, just what you choose to make it; either commonplace, easy and requiring only extensive industry to be lucrative, or else distinguished, difficult and exacting the fiercest intensive industry in return, after a probation of twenty years or so, for authority, reputation and an income only sufficient for simple habits and plain living. The whole professional world lies between these two extremes. At the one, you have the man to whom his profession is only a means of making himself and his family comfortable and prosperous: at the other, you have the man who sacrifices everything and everybody, himself included, to the perfection of his work—to the passion for efficiency which is the true masterpassion of the artist ✦ At the one, work is a necessary evil and moneymaking a pleasure; at the other, work is the objective realization of life and moneymaking a nuisance. At the one, men drink and drug to make themselves comfortable; at the other, to stimulate their working faculty ๑, Preach mere abstinence to the one, and you are preaching nothing but diminution of happiness. Preach it to the other, and you are proposing a reduction of efficiency ✦ If you are to prevail, you must propose a substitute. And the only one I have yet been able to hit on is—going to church.

III

T will not be disputed, I presume, that an unstimulated saint can work as hard, as long, as finely and, on occasion, as fiercely, as a stimulated sinner. Recuperation, recreation, inspiration seem to come to the saint far more surely than to the man who grows coarser and fatter with every additional hundred a year, and who calls the saint an ascetic. A comparison of the works of our carnivorous drunkard poets with those of Shelley, or of Dr. Johnson's dictionary with that of the vegetarian Littre, is sufficient to show that the secret of attaining the highest eminence either in poetry or in dictionary compiling (and all fine literature lies between the two), is to be found neither in alcohol nor in our monstrous habit of bringing millions of useless and disagreeable animals into existence for the express purpose of barbarously slaughtering them, roasting their corpses and eating them. I have myself tried the experiment of not eating meat or drinking tea, coffee or spirits for more than a dozen years past, without, as far as I can discover, placing myself at more than my natural disadvantages relatively to those colleagues of mine who patronize the slaughterhouse and the distillery.

BUT then I go to church. If you should chance to see, in a country church-yard, a bicycle leaning against a tombstone, you are not unlikely to find me inside the church if it is old enough or new enough to be fit for its purpose. There I find rest without languor and recreation without excitement, both of a quality unknown to the traveller who turns from the village church to the village inn and ⁓ seeks to renew himself with shandygaff. Any place where men dwell, village or city, is a reflection of the consciousness of every single man. In my consciousness there is a market, a garden, a dwelling, a workshop, a lover's walk—above all, a cathedral.

MY appeal to the master-builder is : Mirror this cathedral for me in enduring stone; make it with hands ; let it direct its sure and clear appeal to my senses, so that when my spirit is vaguely groping after an elusive mood my eye shall be caught by the skyward tower, showing me where, within the cathedral, I may find my way to the cathedral within me. With

TO CHURCH.

a right knowledge of this great function of the cathedral builder, and craft
enough to set an arch on a couple of
pillars, make doors and windows in a
good wall and put a roof over them,
any modern man might, it seems to
me, build churches as they built them
in the middle ages, if only the pious
founders and the parson would let
him ॐ
For want of that knowledge, gentle-
men of Mr. Pecksniff's profession
make fashionable pencil drawings,
presenting what Mr. Pecksniff's cre-
ator elsewhere calls an architectoor-
alooral appearance, with which, hav-
ing delighted the darkened eyes of the
committee and the clerics, they have
them translated into bricks and masonry and take a shilling in the pound
on the bill, with the result that the
bishop may consecrate the finished
building until he is black in the face
without making a real church of it.
Can it be doubted by the pious that
babies baptized in such places go to

limbo if they die before qualifying themselves for other regions; that prayers said there do not count; nay, that such purposeless, respectable-looking interiors are irreconcilable with the doctrine of Omnipresence, since the bishop's blessing is no spell of black magic to imprison Omnipotence in a place that must needs be intolerable to Omniscience?

T all events, the godhead in me, certified by the tenth chapter of St. John's Gospel to those who will admit no other authority, refuses to enter these barren places. This is perhaps fortunate, since they are generally kept locked; and even when they are open, they are jealously guarded in the spirit of that Westminster Abbey verger who, not long ago, had a stranger arrested for kneeling down, and explained, when remonstrated with, that if that sort of thing were tolerated, they would soon have people praying all over the place. Happily, it is not so everywhere. You may now ride or tramp into a village with a fair chance of finding the church-door open and a manuscript placard in the porch, whereby the parson, speaking no less as a man and a brother than as the porter of the House Beautiful, gives you to understand that the church is open always for those who have any use for it.

INSIDE such churches you will often find not only care-fully cherished work from the ages of faith, which you expect to find noble and lovely, but sometimes a quite modern furnishing of the interior and draping of the altar, evidently done, not by contract with a firm celebrated for its illustrated catalogues, but by some one who loved and understood the church, and who, when baffled in the search for beautiful things, had at least suc-ceeded in avoiding indecently com-mercial and incongruous ones. And then the search for beauty is not always baffled ✦ When the dean and chapter of a cathedral want not merely an ugly but a positively beastly pulpit to preach from—something like the Albert Memorial canopy, only much worse—they always get it, improbable and unnatural as the enterprise is. Similarly, when an enlightened country parson wants an unpretending tub to thump, with a few pretty panels in it and a pleasant shape generally, he will, with a little perseverance, soon enough find a craftsman who has picked up the thread of the tradition of his craft from the time when that craft was a fine art—as may be done nowadays more easily than was possible before we had cheap trips and cheap photographs—and who is only too glad to be allowed to try his hand at something in the line of that tradition.

DURING a bicycle tour, some months ago, I came upon a little church, built long before the sense of beauty and devotion had been supplanted by the sense of respectability and talent, in which some neat panels left by a modern carver had been painted with a few saints on gold backgrounds, evidently by some woman who had tried to learn what she could from the early Florentine masters and had done the work in the true votive spirit, without any taint of the amateur exhibiting his irritating and futile imitations of the celebrated artist business. From such humble but quite acceptable efforts, up to the masterpiece in stained glass by William Morris and Burne-Jones which occasionally astonishes you in places far more remote and unlikely than Birmingham or Oxford, convincing evidence may be picked up here and there that the decay of religious art from the sixteenth century to the nineteenth was not caused by any atrophy of the artistic faculty, but was an eclipse of religion by science and commerce.

T is an odd period to look back on from the church-goer's point of view—those eclipsed centuries calling their predecessors "the dark ages," and trying to prove their own piety by raising, at huge expense, gigantic monuments in enduring stone (not very enduring, though, sometimes) of their infidelity. Go to Milan, and join the rush of tourists to its petrified christening-cake of a cathedral. The projectors of that costly ornament spared no expense to prove that their devotion was ten times greater than that of the builders of San Ambrogio. But every pound they spent only recorded in marble that their devotion was a hundred times less ❧ Go on to Florence and try San Lorenzo, a really noble church (which the Milan Cathedral is not), Brunelleschi's masterpiece. You cannot but admire its intellectual command of form, its unaffected dignity, its power and accomplishment, its masterly combination

TO CHURCH.

of simplicity and homogeneity of plan
with elegance and variety of detail :
you are even touched by the retention
of that part of the beauty of the older
time which was perceptible to the
Renascent intellect before its wean-
ing from heavenly food had been fol-
lowed by starvation. You understand
the deep and serious respect which
Michael Angelo had for Brunelleschi
—why he said " I can do different
work, but not better." But a few minutes' walk to Santa Maria Novella or
Santa Croce, or a turn in the steam-
tram to San Miniato, will bring you
to churches built a century or two
earlier; and you have only to cross
their thresholds to feel, almost before
you have smelt the incense, the dif-
ference between a church built to the
pride and glory of God (not to men-
tion the Medici) and one built as a
sanctuary shielded by God's presence
from pride and glory and all the other
burdens of life. In San Lorenzo up
goes your head—every isolating ad-

vantage you have of talent, power or rank asserts itself with thrilling poignancy.

IN the older churches you forget yourself, and are the equal of the beggar at the door, standing on ground made holy by that labour in which we have discovered the reality of prayer. You may also hit on a church like the Santissima Annunziata, carefully and expensively brought up to date, quite in our modern church-restoring manner, by generations of princes chewing the cud of the Renascence; and there you will see the worship of glory and the self-sufficiency of intellect giving way to the display of wealth and elegance as a guarantee of social importance—in another word, snobbery.

In later edifices you see how intellect, finding its worshippers growing colder, had to abandon its dignity and cut capers to attract attention, giving the grotesque, the eccentric, the baroque, even the profane and blasphemous, until, finally, it is thoroughly snubbed out of its vulgar attempts at self-assertion, and mopes conventionally in our modern churches of St. Nicholas Without and St. Walker Within, locked up, except at service time, from week's end to week's end without ever provoking the smallest protest from a public only too glad to have an excuse for not going into them. You may read the same history of the human soul in any art you like to select; but he who runs may read it in the streets by looking at the churches.

IV

CONSIDER for a moment the prodigious increase of the population of Christendom since the church of San Zeno Maggiore was built at Verona, in the twelfth and thirteenth centuries. Let a man go and renew himself for half an hour occasionally in San Zeno, and he need eat no corpses, nor drink any drugs or drams to sustain him. Yet not even all Verona, much less all Europe, could resort to San Zeno in the thirteenth century; whereas, in the nineteenth, a thousand perfect churches would be but as a thousand drops of rain on Sahara. Yet in London, with near five millions of people in it, how many perfect or usable churches are there? And of the few we have, how many are apparent to the wayfarer? Who, for instance, would guess from the repulsive exterior of Westminster Abbey that there are beautiful chapels and a noble nave within, or cloisters without, on the hidden side?

I REMEMBER, a dozen or so years ago, Parson Shuttleworth, of St. Nicholas Cole Abbey in the city, tried to persuade the city man to spend his mid-day hour of rest in church; guaranteeing him immunity from sermons, prayers and collections, and even making the organ discourse Bach and

TO CHURCH.

Wagner, instead of Goss and Jackson.
This singular appeal to a people walking in darkness was quite successful:
the mid-day hour is kept to this day;
but Parson Shuttleworth has to speak
for five minutes—by general and in-
sistent request—as Housekeeper, al-
though he has placed a shelf of books
in the church for those who would
rather read than listen to him or the
organ ✦ This was a good thought;
for all inspired books should be read
either in church or on the eternal
hills. St. Nicholas Cole Abbey makes
you feel, the moment you enter it,
that you are in a rather dingy rococo
banqueting room, built for a city com-
pany. Corpulence and comfort are
written on every stone of it. Consid-
ering that money is dirt cheap now
in the city, it is strange that Mr. Shuttleworth cannot get twenty thousand
pounds to build a real church ✦ He
would, soon enough, if the city knew
what a church was. The twenty thousand pounds need not be wasted,

either, on a professional "architect."

WHILE lately walking in a polite suburb of New Castle, I saw a church—a new church—with, of all things, a detached campanile; at sight of which I could not help exclaiming profanely: "How the deuce did you find your way to New Castle?" So I went in and, after examining the place with much astonishment, addressed myself to the sexton, who happened to be about. I asked him who built the church, and he gave me the name of Mr. Mitchell, who turned out, however, to be the pious founder—a shipbuilder prince, with some just notion of his princely function. But this was not what I wanted to know; so I asked who was the—the word stuck in my throat a little—the architect. He, it appeared, was one Spence. "Was that marble carving in the altar and that mosaic decoration round the chancel part of his design?" said I. "Yes," said the sexton, with a certain surliness as if he suspected me of disapproving. " The ironwork is good," I remarked, to appease him; " who did that?" " Mr. Spence did." " Who carved that wooden figure of St. George?" (the patron saint of the edifice). " Mr. Spence did." " Who painted those four panels in the dado with figures in oil?" " Mr. Spence did: he meant them to be at intervals round the church, but we put them all together by mistake." " Then, perhaps, he designed the stained windows, too?" " Yes, most of 'em." I got so irritated at this—feeling that Spence was going too far—that I remarked sarcastically that no doubt Mr. Spence designed Mr. Mitchell's ships as well, which turned out to be the case as far as the cabins were concerned.

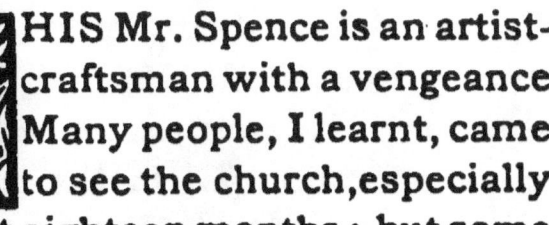

HIS Mr. Spence is an artist-craftsman with a vengeance Many people, I learnt, came to see the church, especially in the first eighteen months; but some of the congregation thought it too ornamental. (At St. Nicholas Cole Abbey, by the way, some of the parishioners objected at first to Mr. Shuttleworth as being too religious.) Now, as a matter of fact, this Newcastle church of St. George's is not ornamental enough. Under modern commercial conditions, it is impossible to get from the labour in the building trade that artistic quality in the actual masonry which makes a good mediæval building independent of applied ornament ❧ Wherever Mr. Spence's artist's hand has passed over the interior surface, the church is beautiful. Why should his hand not pass over every inch of it? It is true, the complete finishing of a large church of the right kind has hardly ever been carried through by one man. Sometimes the man has died; more often the money has failed. But in this instance the man is not dead; and surely money cannot fail in the most fashionable suburb of Newcastle ❧ The

26

chancel with its wonderful mosaics, the baptistry with its ornamental stones, the four painted panels of the dado, are only samples of what the whole interior should and might be. All that cold contract masonry must be redeemed, stone by stone, by the travail of the artist-churchmaker. Nobody, not even an average respectable Sabbathkeeper, will dare to say then that it is over-decorated, however out of place in it he may feel his ugly Sunday clothes and his wife's best bonnet.

HOWBEIT, this church of St. George's in New Castle proves my point, namely, that churches fit for their proper use can still be built by men who follow the craft of Orcagna instead of the profession of Mr Pecksniff, and built cheaply, too; for I took the pains to ascertain what this large church cost, and found that £30,000 was well over the mark. For aught I know, there may be dozens of such churches rising in the country; for Mr. Spence's talent, though evidently a rare and delicate one, cannot be unique, and what he has done in his own style other men can do in theirs, if they want to, and are given the means by those who can make money, and are capable of the same want.

HERE is still one serious obstacle to the use of churches on the very day when most people are best able and most disposed to visit them. I mean, of course, the services. When I was a little boy, I was compelled to go to church on Sunday; and though I escaped from that intolerable bondage before I was ten, it prejudiced me so violently against churchgoing that twenty years elapsed before, in foreign lands and in pursuit of works of art, I became once more a churchgoer. To this day, my flesh creeps when I recall that genteel suburban Irish Protestant church, built by Roman Catholic workmen who would have considered themselves damned had they crossed its threshold afterwards. Every separate stone, every pane of glass, every fillet of ornamental ironwork—half-dog-collar, half-coronet—in that building must have sowed a separate evil passion in my young heart ❧ Yes ; all the vulgarity, savagery, and bad blood which has marred my literary work, was certainly laid upon me in that house of Satan !

OW the mere nullity of the building could make no positive impression on me ; but what could, and did, were the unnaturally motionless figures of the congregation in their Sunday clothes and bonnets, and their set faces, pale with the malignant rigidity produced by the suppression of all expression. And yet these people were always moving and watching one another by stealth, as convicts communicate with one another. So was I. I had been told to keep my restless little limbs still all through those interminable hours; not to talk; and, above all, to be happy and holy there and glad that I was not a wicked little boy playing in the fields instead of worshipping God. I hypocritically acquiesced; but the state of my conscience may be imagined, especially as I implicitly believed that all the rest of the congregation were perfectly sincere and good. I remember at that time dreaming one night that I was dead and had gone to heaven.

ND the picture of heaven which the efforts of the then Established Church of Ireland had conveyed to my childish imagination, was a waiting room with walls of pale sky-coloured tabbinet, and a pew-like bench running all round, except at one corner, where there was a door. I was, somehow, aware that God was in the next room, accessible through that door. I was seated on the bench with

30

TO CHURCH.

my ankles tightly interlaced to prevent my legs dangling, behaving myself with all my might before the grown-up people, who all belonged to the Sunday congregation, and were either sitting on the bench as if at church or else moving solemnly in and out as if there were a dead person in the house. A grimly-handsome lady who usually sat in a corner seat near me in church, and whom I believed to be thoroughly conversant with the arrangements of the Almighty, was to introduce me presently into the next room—a moment which I was supposed to await with joy and enthusiasm.

REALLY, of course, my heart sank like lead within me at the thought; for I felt that my feeble affectation of piety could not impose on Omniscience, and that one glance of that all-searching eye would discover that I had been allowed to come to heaven by mistake ✀ Unfortunately for the interest of this narrative, I awoke, or wandered off into another dream, before the critical moment arrived. But it goes far enough to show that I was by no means an insusceptible subject; indeed, I am sure, from other early experiences of mine, that if I had been turned loose in a real church, and allowed to wander and stare about, or hear noble music there instead of that most accursed Te Deum of Jackson's and a senseless droning of the Old Hundredth, I should never have seized the opportunity of a great evangelical revival, which occurred when I was still in my teens, to begin my literary career with a letter to the Press (which was duly printed), announcing with inflexible materialistic logic, and to the extreme horror of my respectable connections, that I was an atheist.

WHEN, later on, I was led to the study of the economic basis of the respectability of that and similar congregations, I was inexpressibly

TO CHURCH.

relieved to find that it represented a mere passing phase of industrial confusion, and could never have substantiated its claims to my respect if, as a child, I had been able to bring it to book ❧ To this very day, whenever there is the slightest danger of my being mistaken for a votary of the blue tabbinet waiting-room or a supporter of that morality in which wrong and right, base and noble, evil and good, really mean nothing more than the kitchen and the drawing-room, I hasten to claim honourable exemption, as atheist and socialist, from any such complicity.

V

SO when I at last took to church-going again, a kindred difficulty beset me, especially in Roman Catholic countries. In Italy, for instance, churches are used in such a way that priceless pictures become smeared with filthy tallow soot, and have sometimes to be rescued by the temporal power and placed in national galleries. But worse than this are the innumerable daily services which disturb the truly religious visitor. If these were decently and intelligently conducted by genuine mystics to whom the Mass was no mere rite or miracle, but a real communion, the celebrants might reasonably claim a place in the church as their share of the common human right to its use ❧ But the average Italian priest, personally uncleanly, and with chronic catarrh of the nose and throat, produced and maintained by sleeping and living in frowsy, ill-ventilated rooms, punctuating his gabbled Latin only by expectorative hawking, and making the decent guest sicken and shiver and long for sermons in stone, green fields and temples not made with hands; this unseemly wretch of a priest should be seized and put out, bell, book, candle and all, until he learns to behave himself.

TO CHURCH.

HE English tourist is often lectured for his inconsiderate behaviour in Italian ♣ churches, for walking about during service, talking loudly, thrusting himself rudely between a worshipper and an altar to examine a painting, even for stealing chips of stone and scrawling his name on statues. But as far as the mere disturbance of the service is concerned, and the often very evident disposition of the tourist—especially the experienced tourist—to regard the priest and his congregation as troublesome intruders, a week spent in Italy will convince any unprejudiced person that this is a perfectly reasonable attitude. I have seen inconsiderate British behaviour often enough both in church and out of it. The slow-witted Englishman who refuses to get out of the way of the Host, and looks at the bellringer going before it with "Where the devil are you shoving to?" written in every pucker of his free-born

35

British brow, is a familiar figure to me ; but I have never seen any stranger behave so insufferably as the officials of the church habitually do.

IT is the sacristan who teaches you, when once you are committed to tipping him, not to waste your good manners on kneeling worshippers who are snatching a moment from their daily round of drudgery and starvation to be comforted by the Blessed Virgin or one of the saints; it is the officiating priest who makes you understand that the congregation are past shocking by any indecency that you would dream of committing, and that the black looks of the congregation are directed at the foreigner and the heretic only, and imply a denial of your right as a human being to your share of the use of the church. That right should be unflinchingly asserted on all proper occasions ✦ I know no contrary right by which the great Catholic churches made for the

36

TO CHURCH.

world by the great church-builders
should be monopolized by any sect as
against any man who desires to use
them.

Y own faith is clear: I am
a resolute Protestant; I believe in the Holy Catholic
Church; in the Holy Trin-
ity of Father, Son (or Mother, Daugh-
ter) and Spirit; in the Communion of
Saints, the Life to Come, the Immac-
ulate Conception, and the everyday
reality of Godhead and the Kingdom
of Heaven. Also I believe that salva-
tion depends on redemption from belief in miracles; and I regard St.
Athanasius as an irreligious fool—
that is, in the only serious sense of
the word, a damned fool. I pity the
poor neurotic who can say, "Man
that is born of a woman hath but a
short time to live, and is full of mis-
ery," as I pity a maudlin drunkard;
and I know that the real religion of
to-day was made possible only by the
materialist-physicists a n d atheist-

critics who performed for us the indispensable preliminary operation of purging us thoroughly of the ignorant and vicious superstitions which were thrust down our throats as religion in our helpless childhood.

N O W those who assume that our churches are the private property of their sect would think of this profession of faith of mine I need not describe. But am I, therefore, to be denied access to the place of spiritual recreation which is my inheritance as much as theirs? If, for example, I desire to follow a good old custom by pledging my love to my wife in the church of our parish, why should I be denied due record in the registers unless she submits to have a moment of deep feeling made ridiculous by the reading aloud of the naive impertinences of St. Peter, who, on the subject of Woman, was neither Catholic nor Christian, but a boorish Syrian fisherman.

TO CHURCH.

F I want to name a child in the church, the prescribed service may be more touched with the religious spirit— once or twice beautifully touched— but, on the whole, it is time to dismiss our prayer-book as quite rotten with the pessimism of the age which produced it. In spite of the stolen jewels with which it is studded, an age of strength and faith and noble activity can have nothing to do with it: Caliban might have constructed such a ritual out of his own terror of the supernatural, and such fragments of the words of the saints as he could dimly feel some sort of glory in

My demand will now be understood without any ceremonious formulation of it. No nation, working at the strain we face, can live cleanly without public houses of some sort in which to seek rest, refreshment and recreation. To supply that vital want we have the drinking-shop with its narcotic, stimulant poisons, the conventicle with its brimstone-flavoured hot gospel, and the church.

IN the church alone can our need be truly met, nor even there save when we leave outside the door the materializations that help us to believe the incredible, and the intellectualizations that help us to think the unthinkable, completing the refuse-heap of "isms" and creeds with our vain lust for truth and happiness, and going in without thought or belief or prayer or any other vanity, so that the soul, freed from all that crushing lumber, may open all its avenues of life to the holy air of the true Catholic Church.

SO HERE THEN ENDETH THE
PREACHMENT ❧ ON GOING TO
CHURCH ❧ BY GEORGE BER-
NARD SHAW ❦ DONE INTO
PRINT BY ELBERT HUBBARD
AT THE ROYCROFT PRINTING
SHOP WHICH IS IN EAST AU-
RORA, NEW YORK, U. S. A. ❦